British Library Cataloguing in Publication Data

Butterworth, Nick
The school trip.
I. Title II. Inkpen, Mick
823'.914 [J]

ISBN 0-340-51259-8

Copyright © Nick Butterworth and Mick Inkpen 1990

First published 1990

Published by Hodder and Stoughton Children's Books,
a division of Hodder and Stoughton Ltd,
Mill Road, Dunton Green, Sevenoaks, Kent TN13 2YA

Printed in Italy by L.E.G.O., Vicenza

The School Trip

Nick Butterworth and Mick Inkpen

HODDER AND STOUGHTON

London Sydney Auckland Toronto

'Hurry!' says Sam. 'The coach is here!'

'Don't rush,' says Mum. 'There's plenty of time.'

Today is the day of the school trip. Tracy and Sam are going to a big museum. Mum has given them some money to spend in the museum shop.

Tracy is taking her new birthday camera.

'Dad says I can use up a whole film,' she tells her friend.

Mrs Jefferson is sitting in the seat behind the driver, ticking off names. She looks different today in her anorak and trousers.

'Can I take a picture of you, Mrs Jefferson?' asks Tracy.

Sam's friends have saved him a place on the back seat. They are busy huffing on the big back window and drawing faces with their fingers.

Sam waves out of the window and writes in back-to-front letters, 'Goodbye Mum.'

A ll the names have been ticked. All except for Matthew Tibbs.

'Has anyone seen Matthew Tibbs today?' asks Mrs Jefferson.
Nobody has.

'If he's not here soon we'll have to leave without him.'

'There's always one,' says the driver without looking up from his newspaper.

Tracy is practising with her camera. Through the lens she can see someone dawdling up the street.

It's Matthew Tibbs.

The coach rolls through the side streets and out onto the fast main road. Sam and his friends open their lunchboxes.

'I'll swap one of my chocolate biscuits for your crisps,' says Richard.

Joanne has already eaten everything except her apple. But not Henry. Henry doesn't feel well.

'Take deep breaths.'

'Try closing your eyes.'

'Blow into a paper bag.'

But Henry just sits quietly holding the plastic bag that his mum has given him. Just in case.

Hooray! We're here at last. Everyone gets off the coach and lines up. In the entrance to the museum is a grizzly bear. Mary looks nervously at him.

'He won't bite you', says Miss Foster. 'He's only an old stuffed bear.'

But Mary is not so sure. She holds Miss Foster's hand as she goes past.

Sam stands under the bear's paws.

'Take a picture, Tracy,' he says.

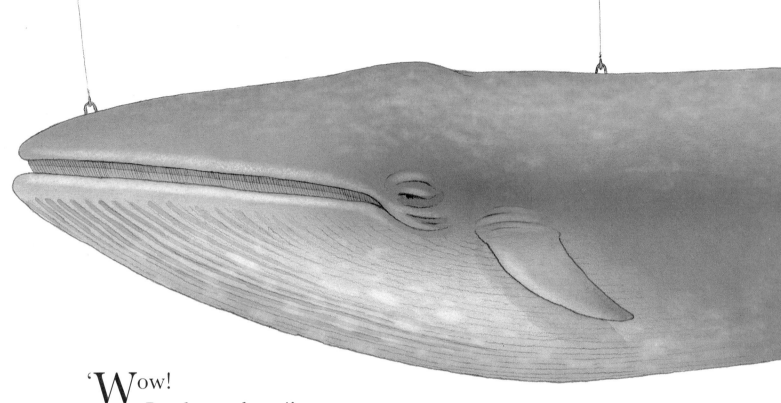

'Wow!
Look up there!'
Above their heads is a full-size model of a blue whale.
It is hanging from the ceiling on thin wires.

'The blue whale is the largest animal that has ever
lived. It weighs as much as twenty-five bull elephants,'
says the plaque.

Tracy can't get it all in, so she takes a photograph
of each end. Click! Click!

Nicola and her friend are looking for buttons to press. They have discovered a room full of electronic screens. Nicola starts one that lights up a picture of a skeleton.

'Bet you can't turn all the others on before it goes out!' says Nicola's friend.

'Bet I can!' says Nicola. And she races round the room pressing buttons.

The attendant doesn't seem to notice. He's seen it all before.

At lunchtime Mrs Jefferson marches everyone into the museum gardens. Henry opens his lunchbox.

'Can I sit next to you, Henry?' says Joanne. She likes the look of Henry's lunch.

Tracy is trying to take a picture of the pigeons, but they keep moving.

Sam and Richard have found a pair of stone lions.

'Come down off there!' says Mrs Jefferson. The woman at the kiosk hands her a cup of tea.

'I expect you could do with this,' she says.

After lunch Mrs Jefferson leads the way to the Dinosaur Room.

'Can anyone tell me, what kind of food did Tyrannosaurus Rex eat?'

She is pointing to a large fossil skull. Its jaws are big enough to sit inside.

Matthew Tibbs pretends to give Tyrannosaurus Rex the remains of his banana.

'No, Matthew,' says Mrs Jefferson, 'Tyrannosaurus Rex was a carnivore. That means he would leave the banana and eat you!'

'Now, for your project I want each of you to choose a dinosaur and draw it,' says Mrs Jefferson. 'No, Mary. You may not draw a bunny rabbit. Bunny rabbits are not dinosaurs, are they?'

Sam is good at drawing. He has done a fine drawing of a diplodocus and another one of Tyrannosaurus Rex eating Matthew Tibbs.

'I think it would spit him out!' says Tracy.

'The coach leaves in twenty minutes,' says
      Miss Foster. 'Now's your chance to visit
the museum shop.'

Tracy buys a beetle brooch with her money.

Sam buys a postcard with a picture of
      a pterodactyl, a rubber tarantula and
      a little fossil.

'It's real,' he tells Tracy.
'Mrs Jefferson says it's nearly as old
as she is.' Mrs Jefferson is good at jokes.

It is time to go home. Mrs Jefferson calls the names.
But when she gets to Matthew Tibbs, there is no answer.

'Oh not again!' she sighs, 'Where is he now?'
But it is alright. Matthew Tibbs is fast asleep in his seat.
It has been a long day.

Tracy has just one picture left.

'Would you take a picture of us all, Miss Foster?' she says.

'Look this way, everyone,' says Miss Foster. 'Say cheese!'
The driver starts the engine.

Matthew Tibbs opens his eyes, then
closes them again. He is dreaming
of a dinosaur called Rex who likes
bananas, cheese and little boys.